Adapted by Mary Man-Kong
Illustrated by Priscilla Wong

 A GOLDEN BOOK • NEW YORK

DreamWorks Trolls © 2016 DreamWorks Animation LLC. All Rights Reserved. Published in the United States by Golden Books, an imprint of Random House Children's Books, a division of Penguin Random House LLC, 1745 Broadway, New York, NY 10019, and in Canada by Penguin Random House Canada Limited, Toronto, in conjunction with DreamWorks Animation LLC. Golden Books, A Golden Book, A Little Golden Book, the G colophon, and the distinctive gold spine are registered trademarks of Penguin Random House LLC.

randomhousekids.com

ISBN 978-0-399-55893-1 (trade) — ISBN 978-0-399-55894-8 (ebook)

Printed in the United States of America
10 9 8 7 6 5 4 3

Once upon a time, in a happy forest filled with happy trees, there lived the happiest creatures the world had ever known: the Trolls. They loved nothing more than to

and dance

sing

and hug

and sing
and dance
and hug—

a lot.

Today was an especially happy day in Troll Village.
Princess Poppy was going to throw a big party!

Everyone was excited to celebrate—except Branch. He didn't like singing, dancing, or hugging. Instead, he spent his time worrying about the Bergens.

Long ago, the Bergens had captured Trolls and eaten them! The Bergens thought that eating Trolls brought them happiness. Luckily, many of the Trolls had escaped . . .

. . . until now.

Princess Poppy's celebration was the biggest, loudest, craziest party ever! It was so loud that the Bergen Chef found where the Trolls had been living all these years.

Most of the

TROLLS

managed to hide.

But Chef was able to scoop up several of them, including Poppy's closest friends, Satin and Chenille, Cooper, Biggie, Guy Diamond, Smidge, DJ Suki, and Creek.

Chef couldn't wait to bring the tasty Trolls back to Bergen Town.

Poppy had to save her friends!
She convinced Branch to help her.

The sooner we get
to Bergen Town, the
sooner we can rescue
everybody and make
it home safely!

Of course, Poppy's plan included making a scrapbook
page—with plenty of glitter!

Meanwhile, thanks to Chef, King Gristle would
finally get to eat a Troll—and experience happiness!
The king decided to have a big celebration called
Trollstice so all the Bergens could eat Trolls and
become happy, too.

When Poppy and Branch got to King Gristle's castle, they found most of their friends hidden in a cage in Bridget the maid's room.

King Gristle will never love me!

But Creek was missing. Bridget agreed to help them find Creek if they could get King Gristle to notice her.

Poppy knew what to do. Satin and Chenille
made Bridget a glitter jumpsuit. Then all the Trolls
sat on her head to make a SUPER-COLORFUL
RainbOW Wig.

Bridget loved her makeover. She
called herself Lady Glittersparkles.
The king would certainly notice her now!

When King Gristle saw Lady Glittersparkles, he fell in love. He didn't realize she was his maid. The king took her roller-skating.

He showed her his new locket.

Creek was inside it!

Later, the Trolls snuck into the king's room to save Creek. They grabbed the locket and

ZOOMED PAST the king,

his pet,

and his guards.

But when Poppy opened the locket, Creek wasn't there! Poppy was sad to learn that to save his own life, Creek had told Chef where all the other Trolls of Troll Village were hiding.

How could Creek have betrayed his friends?

Then everyone was trapped in a pot! Poppy lost all hope, and her color started to FADE.

The other Trolls lost their color, too—they turned gray with sadness.

Suddenly, they heard a beautiful voice singing.
It was Branch! His singing brought out his true colors—
he turned bright green with purple hair.

He sang because his heart was full of the hope and
joy that Poppy had showed him. He loved Poppy, and
Poppy loved Branch. She and the other Trolls started
to sing, too, and their true colors came back.

Bridget couldn't let the Bergens eat her friends.
She lifted the cover off the pot so the Trolls could
escape. Bridget knew she would get in trouble, but
she was glad she'd had one day of happiness
on her date with the king.

At Trollstice, the Bergens, eager to finally get a taste of happiness, were angry to discover that Bridget had set the Trolls free.

Just then, the Trolls burst in to save her. They formed the **RAINBOW WIG** again . . .

. . . and landed right on Bridget's head.

When King Gristle learned that Lady Glittersparkles was actually Bridget, he was overjoyed. He realized that he didn't need to eat a Troll to be happy.

All he needed was a full heart and Bridget by his side. "They do look kind of happy," one Bergen admitted.

Branch told everyone how miserable he'd been until Poppy had taught him how to dance and hug and sing. Before long, all the Bergens were dancing and singing, too.

The only Bergen who wasn't happy was Chef. Now that no one wanted to eat Trolls, she was out of a job! Chef and Creek were banished from Bergen Town, destined to be unhappy together.

The Trolls had brought happiness to Bergen Town, but not in a way anyone had expected. The Trolls had a huge celebration. Poppy was crowned queen of the Trolls, and everyone cheered.

After finally experiencing their true colors, the Bergens and the Trolls now lived in peaceful harmony.